THE MENTOR 1 - A BAD INFLUENCE

From House Wife To Hotwife

ALLORA SINCLAIR

Cuckoo
Publishing

THE MENTOR 1 - A BAD INFLUENCE

©2021 by Allora Sinclair

Front Cover Illustration by: Chaoss

To Helen, your love, inner strength and wisdom have meant the world to me.

CHAPTER ONE

The room was filled with dozens of sweaty, hot, sexy women. All dressed in next to nothing. This was Anna's first visit to a gym. She attempted to regain some confidence. Turning 40 did a number on her self-esteem. Being married for just over seven years and having two kids, she could feel her sex appeal was all but dead. She was sure getting in shape would help.

"Okay ladies, let's work those glutes. And one, and two, and..."

The instructor at the front of the class was ridiculously fit. She was half the age of most of the women. All Anna could think about was how much of a mistake coming was. Who did she think she was? She was no spring chicken anymore. Sure, she still had a nice body, but she was 40. Middle-aged. The beginning of the end of being a sexy, vibrant woman.

A glance at the wall clock told her there was still

another 20 minutes to the class. Looking good was easy. Being fit, not so much. She hated every second and her face said nothing different.

She noticed she was not alone in the way she felt. Quickly scanning the room, most of the other women were in equal amounts of pain. It looked like they were all there against their own will. Except for the woman on the mat behind her. This woman looked like she was loving life, the pain, the whatever.

Anna kept turning around to see if this woman was high or what. No one can like this obnoxious abuse to the body. The woman winked, noticing Anna's admiration. The woman looked about the same age as Anna, but she had an aura about her. She had a synergy, a sort of sexual energy that poured out with every drop of perspiration.

As the class ended, the woman approached Anna and introduced herself.

"Hi there. I noticed you kept turning around. Was I making too much noise?"

Anna felt awkward in how to respond. Her default was to just be honest.

"Hi, I'm Anna. I just noticed you seemed to be the only lady here that was having a good time. What's your secret?"

The woman smiled as a soft laugh came out.

"I have no secret. I hate this place too. I just want to look good for my guys. I'm Julia by the way."

Anna felt relief knowing this other woman was also suffering. Still, there was something about her Anna felt drawn to.

"Okay, good. Because you look like you live for health and fitness," Anna said.

Julia casually walked over to her towel and smirked as she wiped off the excess perspiration.

"Oh, God, no. I just like having fun. And no, this is not fun, but if I don't do this, I'll get fat, and then the fun stops. Listen, are you doing anything now?" Julia said.

"No, nothing at all. My next shift at work isn't till tonight so... Why?"

"Let's go grab a coffee. You look like you could use the pick me up."

The two women left with Julia leading the way. The cafe was one block away, so they walked and left their cars at the gym parking. As they waited at the set of lights to cross, Julia reached into her purse to pull out a long, slim cigarette. Anna turned.

"You smoke? Okay, I guess you were right. You're not a health nut. But you look so good."

Julia smiled as she blew out the smoke.

"Why thank you, Anna. You're not bad yourself. We just need to do a little work on bringing your self-confidence up and you'll be fine. Are you married? You have any kids?"

Wasting no time, Anna dumped her life on to Julia. She did not know why, but something inside her told her this woman was about to become her best friend. They just seemed to connect.

"Yes, on both counts. I'm married and have two kids, a boy, and a girl. What about yourself?" Anna asked.

"Ya, I'm married. How old are your hubby and kids?"

"Robert is 54. My son is 17 and my daughter is 15"

"And what does Robert do?" Julia asked.

"He's a CFO of a large distribution and logistics company. Trifecta. You may have heard of them."

"Wow. Yes, I see their trucks on the highway all the time."

They arrived at the cafe, placed their orders, and found a quiet table outside on the patio. As they continued talking, Anna could not stop herself. Julia kept asking question after question. Each getting more and more personal.

"Anna, you're what 35? How's the sex? I mean, you said your hubby is 54, so I'm assuming it's boring as fuck?"

It floored Anna. This was not something she normally discussed with anyone, including her husband. She could not help smiling as she replayed the dialogue.

"Welllllll. I feel so guilty admitting it but, yes. Robert takes so long to get hard. It can get frustrating. My biggest complaint isn't even his age. I mean, I can deal with that. He's just so... I don't know. And I'm 40, but thanks for the compliment."

Julia saw the chance and jumped in. "Small? Tiny? Like you have more fun when you use your dildo."

It shocked Anna how bold her new friend was being. It also made her feel like she had finally found a woman she could be truly open with who was not judgemental.

"You're terrible, Julia. But okay, yes. Yes, yes, yes. He's friggen small. I would never say that to him though. I feel so bad saying this. I can't believe I'm finally telling someone. And I barely know you."

The two women had a laugh about how quickly they were becoming besties. The conversation turned to discuss their plans for the evening when Anna noticed it was almost 1 pm.

"Holy shit! I gotta go. I'm scheduled to work the afternoon shift this week and I still have to get home to make Robert's dinner before I go."

"Where do you work?" Julia asked.

"I'm an orderly at St. Vincent's Hospital. I know, not the greatest, but it helps subsidize paying for all the toys Robert gets."

"Honey, we need to talk. I realize you need to go now, but let's make a date. You coming to Thursday's workout?"

Anna had planned to ask for a refund on the classes, but this woman had somehow convinced her to try it.

"Yes, I'll be there."

The two women left with Anna feeling both excited and confused about this new friend. She finally had something interesting to share with her husband when he got home.

CHAPTER TWO

*R*acing in the house, Anna threw her car keys on the table and ran upstairs to shower, change and prepare dinner. Her mind was racing as the water rolled down her slim, long legs. Every muscle in her body was in pain. She could not let go of wondering how this woman, Julia, seemed so well put together. And why did she seem to open up so much?

Potatoes peeled, chicken roasting in the oven, and the vegetables slowly cooking on the stove, Anna packed her work dinner and was getting dressed in her hospital scrubs as Robert arrived.

"Hun. I'm upstairs getting ready for work. How was your day?"

She could hear her husband bark some low-volume response, prompting to respond.

"Just give me a minute. I'll be down in a few."

When Anna came downstairs, Robert was sitting on

the couch watching the news feeds from CNN. He hung his suit blazer over the stair rail and his shoes sat haphazardly in the front hall.

"Sorry about that, Hun. I didn't hear how your day went."

Robert maintained his focus on the TV, paying no attention to his wife.

"I SAID IT WAS FINE. When's dinner going to be ready?"

Feeling deflated and somewhat invisible, Anna said, "Um, it should be ready in about 20 minutes. You're not forgetting I'm on afternoons this week?"

"What? Oh, ya. Okay. Listen, babe, can you grab me a beer? I'm exhausted."

Anna quickly lost her enthusiasm to have any conversation at all. She was looking forward to telling Robert about her new friend Julia and the whole work-out class, but her husband seemed more concerned about the latest stocks and futures.

"Sure, dear. You want anything else while I'm in the kitchen?"

"Maybe grab me a bag of chips. I'm starving"

Anna returned with his beer and a bowl of his favorite bbq chips. As she passed both to him, no 'thank you' was given. He still had yet to make eye contact or ask about her day. Sitting beside him on the couch, Anna still wanted to say something, anything about her day.

"So, I went to that aerobics class I told you about. I also met this cool woman, Julia. We went for coffee after the workout."

"Shhh. Can't you see? I'm watching the news here. Can't this wait till later?"

Anna was now getting pissed. This seemed so like Robert. A grumpy old fart.

"Robert, I told you. I'm going to work in an hour. Later is when?"

Muting the TV, he turned to his wife with a blank look of indifference.

"Okay, go ahead. Tell me about your fitness class."

"The class was boring and painful, but this lady I met Julia, She has convinced me to go back in a couple of days."

"That's great. Okay, are we done? Can I go back to the news?" Robert said with contempt.

"Robert, do you love me? I mean, really. We seem so distant from each other. Maybe it's our age difference. Maybe it's catching up to us. There's 15 years difference between us. I just feel like we have nothing in common. You're buried in your work and the boys. It's like I'm just your maid when you arrive home."

Robert did not see this coming. Anna was always a quiet, passive, and agreeable wife.

"Where is this coming from? Of course, I love you. What the hell are you talking about? You're crazy."

Anna did not want this to turn into one of their blow-up, nuclear arguments where ultimately he'd force her to agree and she would go to work feeling like shit.

"I'm not crazy! This is just the stuff I was telling Julia about. As soon as I told her there was a huge age gap, she wondered how we could be compatible."

"Who the hell is Julia?"

"The lady I met at the gym. I've been trying to tell you about my day, but you don't seem to care." Anna said.

"You just met this woman, and you're telling her about my age? That's none of her business."

Anna sensed she had hit a nerve with her husband. For whatever reason, he did not want his wife discussing their personal details with anyone that did not need to know.

"Why would you care I told her our age differences? It turns out her husband, I think she said his name was Frankie or something, he's 17 years her senior. It was just nice to connect with someone that has almost the same situation as ours."

"Situation? What situation. Are you saying I'm an old man and you're with me cause you feel sorry for me?" Robert said as his face turned a deep red.

There it was. Anna could see Robert was nervous. He wanted their age gap to not become 'a thing'.

"Hun, are you insecure about being that much older than me? I love you and I don't care at all. I just thought it was nice to talk to another woman that was in a similar situation." Anna said in a soft and caring tone.

"Well, we've never talked about our ages before and it makes me feel like an old man. I don't like you talking to this Julia chick. What else did you talk about?"

Anna struggled to hold the smile from her face. She was not about to reveal that the two women talked in great detail about the age gap, proving to be an actual issue in the bedroom.

"Just the fitness class and how we both hurt so much. I think you're overreacting. I like Julia. She seems like a real positive force. Anyway, your dinner should be ready."

She left the room feeling frustrated and angry. She could be sensitive to her husband's insecurities but, "don't talk to her again?" That was too much. Unable to hide her annoyance, she slammed the dinner plates on the kitchen counter and yelled the "it's on the table" universal call.

Before Robert sat down, Anna had her work bag and purse slung over her shoulders.

"What the hell? Where are you going?" Robert looking dumb-founded.

"Work! Have a fantastic evening, Robert." Anna said in the driest and most sarcastic voice she could muster.

As she made the hour-long drive downtown, she had time to think.

I wonder why Robert got so upset about me talking about our age gap. I mean, it's not like Julia's not in the same boat. I have to tell her this. I wonder if her husband does the same thing.

CHAPTER THREE

*A*nna arrived early to the gym, picking out a section at the back, so the instructor would avoid any motivational yelling her way. Just as the class was about to begin, Julia came in and placed her mat next to Anna's. Both women were there in body, but it was clear neither of them enjoyed the vim and vigor. No time wasted, Anna turned to Julia as the class ended.

"Coffee?"

"Absolutely!"

They barely left the building when Julia grilled Anna again. The 8-minute walk to the cafe evaporated. The two women seemed to connect like they were long-lost sisters. This felt so good to Anna. She had been feeling so isolated since the kids were seldom home and her husband was the rock star at work.

"So... how did it go?" Julia inquired.

"What do you mean?" Anna trying to play innocent and naïve.

"Your body. How have you survived trying to get back into shape? Why? What did you think I was asking you about?"

Anna blushed. She crossed her arms and sat back, trying to give the illusion that she was cool.

"Anna, talk to me. What did you think I was talking about?"

"Well, you're going to think I'm weird, but I feel connected to you. Like I can tell you anything. I got a little excited that you came into my life and I told my husband about meeting you at the first class."

"Oh. I see. So how did that go?" Julia seemed unsure what the big deal was about.

"I'm not sure. My husband doesn't want me talking to you anymore."

Julia's eyes opened wide as her mouth opened.

"What!? You need permission from your little hubby to make friends?"

"No. He was just pissed that you and I talked about our vast age differences. He got uneasy. I mean, I get it. It kind of reminds him he's... um."

"Say it! Say it, Anna! He's an old man. You're entering the prime of your life and he's on his way out. Wow. I'm shocked that little men like your husband are still out there. Forgive me, but wow."

Julia was only saying what Anna was thinking and feeling. It pissed her off. She just felt so guilty thinking this way about the man she so loved and adored.

Anna avoided eye contact as she spoke.

"I know. He's wrong to tell me who I can and can't

hang out with. I know him well. It's just that he's got this big bravado of being THE MAN and when we talk about his age, it reminds him he's getting old and..."

"And what? By our conversation a couple of days ago, you want to say 'and useless in bed'" Julia said as she pulled her chair out to cross her legs. She dug into her purse and pulled out a cigarette. She offered one to Anna.

"No, I quit smoking when Robert and I started dating. I quit a lot of things when we got together." Anna said.

"Look, you have one life. You come into this world alone. You leave it alone. You need to do what's right for you. You look like you could use one. Here." Julia slowly extracted a second cigarette from the package and handed it to Anna. She then ignited the lighter and leaned into Anna.

As natural as breathing, Anna placed the cigarette to her lips and let the flame dance as the fresh tobacco smoke entered her mouth. As she inhaled, her mouth instantly filled with the strong menthol and tobacco flavors in her mouth. Her lungs felt gently caressed by the soft smoke. As she exhaled, she could feel the rush of nicotine entering her body. She felt so alive. So satisfied.

Julia watched as she could see Anna revisit the sinful pleasure. Her face looked at Anna with sincere happiness and satisfaction. She put the package back in her purse and continued.

"Anna, you seem like a nice girl. But you're not a girl, you're a woman. You need to grow up. Stop being your husband's little puppet. If anything, he should dance around you. Any guy half his age would donate his left testicle to be with you."

Anna was still swimming in the nicotine rush but knew enough to appreciate what Julia was saying.

"I try to be the best wife. I do everything for that man. Cook, clean, do all the shopping and I have this part-time job at the stupid hospital so he has some extra money to buy his new golf clubs. I just keep waiting for him to show some appreciation."

Without letting Anna pause, Julia jumped in.

"FLR. Have you ever heard of it?"

"No. What's that, a medical condition or something?"

"It stands for Female Led Relationship. It is what Fluffy and I are in."

"Fluffy? Who's that?" Anna asked.

"Sorry, I tell everyone his name is Frank or Frankie when we first meet. It's my husband. In our relationship, I call him fluffy."

Anna looked confused and shocked.

"That seems kind of rude and condescending if you ask me."

"It is. It's all part of our FLR life. Let me guess, you have no idea what female led relations is? Do you, little girl?"

The two women spent the next hour and a half delving into the nitty-gritty details of Julia's marriage dynamics. It dumbfounded Anna that such a relationship could exist, never mind that it was a reality with this new friend. The more Julia disclosed, the more Anna enquired. This was so amazing and yet disturbing at the same time. How could this be? Anna thought to herself.

As Anna drove home, she could feel a dampness between her legs. She could not contain herself, she was so excited at the prospect. Was there any chance that Robert would consider this? She felt so guilty for even entertaining the thought. How was her husband going to take this idea when she told him?

CHAPTER FOUR

*S*crambling to get ready for work, Anna made the executive decision to do a quick heat and serve frozen pizza for Robert's arrival. She did not like this gym workout thing but was loving the new friendship. She felt empowered but scared of the reaction she was about to get.

Getting out of the shower, she could hear the thud of the front door closing. Robert had arrived home.

"Hey Hunny, I'm just out of the shower. I'll be down in a few minutes."

The response was silence.

Robert had once again left his sports jacket, shoes, and now briefcase wherever he felt like it. He was a little boy looking for his mommy to clean up after him, Anna thought to herself. She ignored him as she went to the kitchen to place the pizza into the oven. Bending over to kiss him, he muted the TV and turned.

"Have you been smoking?"

Anna did not expect this. Fear ran through her like a child about to be yelled at by their parents.

"Um, why?"

"I said, have you been smoking?"

"No, I have not gone back to smoking. Yes, I had A CIGARETTE. You can smell it even after my shower?"

"The house stinks. I could smell it as soon as I came in. What the hell are you doing?"

The extreme reaction from Robert pushed her over the edge. She was sick of being spoken to and treated like his child.

"I had coffee with Julia after our workout today. She offered me a cigarette and end of story. Listen, we need to talk."

"Damn right we need to talk." Robert then continued, "I told you, I don't want you hanging out with that woman. She is too much of a busybody and now look, she's got you back on cancer sticks. What is your problem?"

Anna sat down, pursed her lips, and looked her husband directly in the eyes.

"Look, Rob. I'm not happy with our life. You treat me like I'm here for your convenience. I do everything for you and in return, you tell me how to live my life. This has to change or our marriage is heading for disaster."

Her husband leaned back and placed his hands behind his head.

"Okay, okay. Relax. Where is this all coming from? It's that workout friend planting these ideas in your head, isn't it?"

Anna stood up and raised her voice. She could feel the years of being the devoted housewife about to explode.

"Listen. I like my new friend. And Julia IS HER NAME. Get used to it. I'm sick of being your personal slave. I've talked to her about how our lives seem to run and she's helped me realize it should not be this way."

Robert broke eye contact and looked at the floor. He moved forward on the couch.

"Why are you being so difficult?" He asked.

"Difficult? What the fuck is difficult about me expressing how I feel. We need to change the rules of our relationship. For the last ten years, it's all been about you. NO MORE! It's my turn."

His lips trembled. Anna could see he was appreciating the gravity of the situation.

"Look, I just want what's best for you, dear." He responded.

"No! That's for me to decide, not you. First things first, I refuse to be a maid. You come home, hang your fucking jacket up and put your shoes where they belong."

"Okay, okay. What's gotten into you?"

"I'm not done. Second, Julia has become a wonderful friend. I plan on seeing her again. You don't get to tell me who I hang out with."

"Fine."

"Third, I think we need to sit down and have a serious heart to heart conversation this weekend. The pizza is almost ready and then I have to go to work. You remembered I'm working tonight?"

Robert stuttered. He had not stuttered since he was a teenager getting bullied in the schoolyard.

"Y y yes, dear. I I I'm s s sorry."

Hearing this come out of her husband, Anna felt sorry for him but also felt like he deserved the retribution.

"I love you, Robert. But I deserve better. I'm taking back the power I once had before we met."

He stood up, walked sheepishly towards her, and gestured they embrace. Her instinct was to oblige, but something deep inside her wanted to see him suffer.

"Not in the mood, Robert. You can't just kiss me and make things all better."

"Okay. I'm listening to you, sweetheart. I will try to go easy on you."

"NO! You still don't get it! It's not about making things easy for me. I am changing. You need to change too. This... whatever this is. It ain't working."

The more aggressive Anna got, the more compliant and timid her husband became.

"So, what do you want me to do?" He asked.

"Right now, I don't know. We both need to think long and hard here. I've gotta go to work. I will see you tomorrow afternoon."

Anna walked out of the room, stormed into the kitchen, and slammed the cooked pizza on the counter. She then grabbed her work bag and walked out of the house without saying another word.

CHAPTER FIVE

7 pm coffee break came faster than Anna expected. Her mind was racing about the conversations she had with both Julia and Robert earlier in the day. Female led relationships. Who would have thought this was possible? She wanted to share with Julia the reaction she had from her husband. Watching her husband stumble as she became aggressive made her feel kind of bad. It also made her realize she is not a puppet. She wanted something more.

Pulling out her phone, she sent Julia a text:

SPOKE TO HUBBY. HE FELL APART. FEEL BAD BUT THINK

YOU ARE RIGHT. I DESERVE MORE. AT WORK NOW BUT WOULD

LOVE TO TALK BEFORE NEXT WORKOUT.

She hit send with the whoop sound as it went off. She

poured herself a coffee and pulled out a granola bar to snack on. Her phone pinged. It was Julia responding.

HELLO DEAR. ANYTHING TO HELP A SISTER. WHAT TIME

DO YOU FINISH YOUR SHIFT? COFFEE AND A SMOKE? (LOL)

Anna smiled as she read the text. This woman made her feel so understood.

She typed:

NOT TILL LATE - 11:30 PM. IKR, TOO LATE :(

Before she could put her phone away, a response came back.

DONE. WHERE AND WHEN?

Wow, this was a true friend. Anna responded, suggesting a coffee shop down the street from the hospital, knowing that Julia also lived in the downtown core. Her phone chirped one last time before returning to her schedule:

CU SOON :)

During the entire walk from the hospital to the cafe, Anna could feel the excitement. Oh, my God. She was actually looking forward to having a smoke. She laughed to herself, feeling that if anyone deserved one right now, it was her. Julia was inside, waiting at a table by the front window.

Anna went directly to the counter and looked over to see Julia had already ordered her a beverage.

"Never mind. My friend has already got me something." Anna said to the barista as she turned to the table. Julia stood up and announced they were both in "to-go" cups.

"Let's go outside. You look like you could use one." As she pulled her package out of her purse.

The two women stood under the scone lights outside as Julia lit.

"So? What happened, Anna?"

"Well, I put my foot down. I told him things had to change. I said nothing about becoming an FLR couple, but you could tell I intimidated him."

Julia looked up to the light above them and smiled.

"Girlfriend, you do not know. I'm just getting started with you."

Anna smiled, assuming she was about to receive some words of wisdom or advice on what to do next. She raised her arms, prompting Julia to elaborate.

"Anna, let me ask. Before you and Rob met, what kind of woman were you? Your two kids, are they his? Clearly, you used to smoke. I mean, were you always a goody goody?"

"My two children are from two other men that I met way before Rob. I was a train wreck. Party girl was my middle name. When I met Rob, I cleaned up my life. I stopped the drugs, the late nights out with who knows how many men. I wanted to bring my kids up in a stable home."

As Anna finished, Julia paced and nodded her head.

"Now it's making total sense, Anna. Does Rob know about your past?"

"Of course he does. I met him in a bar while I was on a bender. He saw that side of me, believe me."

"I see. And these 'changes' you made to yourself. Did they come at the request of your husband?"

Anna reflected. Her daughter was 3 and her son 5.

"Shit, that's over 10 years ago, Julia. I don't think he cared. I just wanted to become the woman he deserved. He has been so good to me and my kids and..."

Julia put her hand up to stop Anna from continuing.

"Okay, dear. Here's what you probably don't realize. Most men love the woman you were. NOT the boring, and unadventurous woman you have made yourself become."

"What? You're crazy, Julia. Robert loves me being his little maid and companion. He does not want party girl Anna."

"You would think. But not so much Anna. I know what I'm talking about. I have many ladies I have mentored over the years. I've seen your situation more times than I could count."

"Mentor? Ok, I'm confused. Are you saying you're trying to mentor me? Mentor me into what? An irresponsible mother and wife?"

"Not at all. I believe women are at the top of the food chain. Men are here to serve. For centuries, our society has trained little girls to be nothing but servants to their men. Not anymore. Female led relationships are the start of turning things around. But there is more. So much more." Julia ended her words with an enormous smile as a seductive stream of smoke exhaled slowly out of her nose.

The two women returned inside the cafe to order another mochaccino. As Julia continued to talk, it drew in Anna with both feet. She liked what she was hearing. Finally, Julia hit the area that had Anna's full attention.

"Take your sex life. You said Robbie is insufficient, lacking stamina and drive. So... why should you have to live with that for the rest of your married life?"

Anna squinted. "It's not like I'm going to cheat on him. That's just plain wrong."

"You're right. Doing that is a loveless marriage."

"So what the hell are you suggesting, Julia?"

"Cuckolding." Julia let the word hang to see if Anna was familiar with the word.

"Cuckolding? Is that some kind of therapy method or something?"

"Not exactly. Let me explain."

It was after two in the morning before the two women recognized it was now too late to attend the morning workout class. Julia had gone into complete detail, explaining the in's and out's of cuckolding. She made it clear to Anna that turning their marriage into an FLR was absolutely the way to go, but also suggested cuckolding her husband may help seal the deal.

"I know it seems crazy at first. But if your Robbie was into you when you were still a 'bad girl', it's because that's what he likes. You've changed who you are to please him, but what if he's the way he is BECAUSE you changed?"

"I don't know. I think he'd lose his shit if I suggested I fuck other guys. I mean really, who the hell does that?" Anna said.

"Way more couples than you think, Anna. The world is changing and changing fast. More and more women recognize the power of female seduction and spirit. We have been kept down for so long by men. I see a new world order and I see a woman at the top. It's only a matter of time."

They both got up to close the conversation when Julia suggested one more smoke for the road as they exited the cafe. As they stood, Julia opened her phone calendar.

"I have an idea. Why don't we have a double date? You and your Robbie and I can bring fluffy. Say dinner at the Ambrosia Rooftop Bar and Restaurant?"

"Oh, I'd love that. We haven't been out for a dinner for a long time."

"Good," Julia responded. "It will give me a chance to check out your little man. I have an amazing nose for sniffing out cucks. We'll talk and I'm going to push some buttons. If I sense you may make a mistake, I'll let you know. If he's a true cuckold, he won't be able to hide from me. Trust me."

CHAPTER SIX

*A*nna was able to convince Rob to a meet-up dinner with only a little objection. For two days, he seemed to have no resistance to any requests Anna made. The heated discussion she had with him a few days previously seemed to sink in more than she thought it would. She sent a quick three-line text to Julia confirming their dinner arrangements. The dinner date was finally upon them. In typical Robert style, they were a full 30 minutes early, waiting in the lobby with uncomfortable silence.

"Oh, there you are, love. You look smashing." Julia exclaimed to Anna as she and her husband entered.

"Hi, Julia. This is my hubby... I mean husband, Robert."

Julia gave Anna a stern look, subtly chastising her for correcting herself to be polite and politically correct.

The four were seated outside, with a panoramic view of the city skyline at dusk. It was breathtaking with the glitz of a vibrant, high energy city. Robert turned discretely to his wife and whispered into Anna's ear.

"This is going to be ridiculously expensive, you know that?"

Anna treated his remark with contempt and carried on talking with Julia's husband, offering no acknowledgment.

"So Robbie, tell me about your big man job as a CFO," Julia said with a seductive smile.

"Well, first, it's Robert." He was outwardly unimpressed with the name distortion. "I've been there for 18 years. Slowly worked my way out of the accounting department and now, I'm the man who says if there is money or not."

"Excellent. Now, Anna tells me your children are actually not yours? That must have been an enormous sacrifice. By your age gap, I take it Anna is not your first wife?"

It floored Robert at how abrasive this woman was being. There was no gentle 'getting to know you' small talk. Straight to the point.

"Um, yes. Our two kids are not mine, biologically. But I love them as my own. And yes, I was married once before. It lasted two years. Huge mistake."

Julia gave Anna a gentle kick under the table to watch where she was about to take the conversation.

"So two wives... and you're what... same age as my Frankie here, 58?"

"No, actually I'm 54. Sorry, Frank" as he turned to the other man who was all but silent during most of the socializing.

"Oh, I see. Well, at least you played the field in your younger days. Sow your wild oats, so to speak? I mean, it must be hard for you to keep up with your dynamo wife here. You should see her in our fitness classes. I've had to practically pull her away from all the guys in every session."

Robert put his head down. He avoided any eye contact with both ladies. His face seemed to go a deep red. Fearing he would lash out, Anna jumped in.

"Hun, you ok?"

Robert looked up, placing both his hands under his legs, and shook his head.

"No, no, I I I'm fine."

Like a badger, Julia jumped in for round two.

"Oh, look at that. I've embarrassed the big man. I'm sorry, Robbie". Julia paused, pouted, and mimicked a mother talking to her infant. "Did I hurt your little feelings?"

As Julia engaged Robert, Anna tried to remain silent. She was not sure what kind of control this other woman had on her husband, but it was tangible. She could feel it in the air. Her husband had become a wimp. As much as it broke her heart, there was some degree of deep satisfaction she didn't understand in herself.

Robert remained quiet for several minutes to recompose his thoughts. He had memorized the place setting layout with his eyes fixated on nothing else. Julia pushed on.

"Look, Anna, somebody has cut little Robbie's tongue off. Are you ok darling? I'm just having fun with you."

"I I I'm fine. Anna w was right. Y You are quite the woman."

That was all Julia needed to hear. She turned to Anna, inviting her to join her in the smoking section as the boys talked about their little boy toys. Anna's face lit up. She could not believe she had found the courage to do this in front of her husband.

"I would love that, Julia. Hun, I'm going for a cigarette. You play nice with Frankie."

The two women giggled as they walked across the terrace to the designated smoking section. Anna busting to say something.

"Well, my dear, I believe you have yourself a soon to be cuckold."

"WHAT?! What makes you think that?" Anna replied.

"I told you, trust me. I just know these things."

"There's no way you can tell that from the insulting way you spoke to him. I'm surprised he didn't lash out at you."

"Exactly my dear. He has remained a good little boy. And I'll tell you why. He loved what I was doing to him. Here's what I'm going to do. I'm going to have him flat out tell you to hang out with me more. LOT'S MORE. If he does it, you know he's a cuck."

As Anna was listening to her new friend, her heart began racing. This woman was evil. She was afraid of her but also wanted to follow in her footsteps . She knew Julia would be right.

"Ok, Julia, let's just see how this plays out."

The two women returned. Not knowing what got into her, Anna felt compelled to kiss her husband directly on the lips where the smell and taste of fresh tobacco lingered. She wanted to rub it in his face. As she sat down beside him, she continued with the boldness of her friend. Discreetly lowering her left hand below the table, she gently placed her hand on Rob's groin. He could not stand up for the tent in his pants. This was interesting, Anna thought to herself.

After the meals were served and enjoyed, Julia called for the server.

"Yes, I'd like to order your most expensive wine, and, you can bring the bill with it. Thanks, Mr. Big."

This was an unexpected turn of events. Anna was unsure where things were going, but she complacently followed Julia's lead.

"Julia, another cigarette?"

"Lovely! You little boys stay here while we socialize with the real men over there. Listen, Robbie, be a darling and take care of the bill while we're gone. C'mon Anna, let's have some lung exercises."

As the two women walked away, Anna turned around to glance back at her husband. She could see the erection under the table.

"This is fun, Julia."

"I'm still not done, Anna."

When the women returned, the bill was paid and a bottle of Dom Perignon rose gold champagne sat in the center of the table. Robert tried to recompose himself with some confidence. That was all Julia wanted to see.

"Robbie, you're such a nice hubby. Just like my little fluffy here." Her hand gesturing to the man sitting beside her.

"I wanted a chance to meet you because your beautiful wife here says you had some problems with me when we first met. Is this true Robbie?"

Having discussed things in advance, Anna moved her hands back to do a quick cock check. Growing and growing fast.

"U Um n n no. I I think you're an amazing woman. I I really like you, Julia."

Julia looked at Anna with a slight tilt.

"Soooo, I think it would be a good thing if your beautiful hot wife and I became best friends.?"

Anna put her unused hand to cover her mouth. She could not believe what was happening. Her husband was rock hard. Harder than she had ever seen.

"Y y yes. I think y you should b be b b best friends."

"Fantastic! So I guess you would want us to hang out A LOT MORE? Is that what Anna and I are hearing you say, little Robbie?"

Anna swore she could feel his pants getting wet with pre-cum. She had to bring her hand up from under the table. He needed time to deflate before they could get up to leave.

"Y yes."

"Don't tell me, tell your wife, dammit!"

He turned to Anna with a hypnotic look in his eyes, like he had just seen God.

"Anna my dear, please please please. I think th th this woman, Julia is is is an amazing per per person. I think it would be wonderful if you spent a lot more time together with her."

Anna smiled devilishly.

"Robbie, I think that's the smartest thing you've said out of your cute little brain in years," Anna responded.

She could not believe she was being so cruel to her husband. She also could not understand why it felt so good and empowering. Not having any idea what the next steps would be, Anna made a coffee date with Julia for the following midday as the two couples left the rooftop.

CHAPTER SEVEN

The drive home started in silence. Rob sat in the passenger seat while Anna waited patiently for any dialogue he would initiate. Approaching the highway exit to their cozy suburban community, she had had enough.

"Robbie, you've said nothing, the entire drive home. What did you think?"

Crouched towards the front dashboard, his shoulders slouched, he was a defeated man looking like he had just lost his job.

"Fine. She seems fine." He said.

"That's it? That's all you have to say is fine?"

Rob's head veered towards Anna, but his eyes refused to make direct contact.

"Um um um, y y yes dear."

Anna could see the spell Julia had cast lingered on both of them. She felt unexplainably powerful. Her husband was still a little baby wanting his little mommy, she thought to herself.

"Yes, what!? Listen, Robbie, I think Julia has had a significant positive impact on my self-confidence and self-esteem. I've been your little puppet and maid long enough. She has made me see what I've allowed myself to become, and tonight it ends."

She looked down, just out of curiosity. There it was. A bulge in his pants. A rush of adrenaline ran through her. Had she been missing this side of her husband all those years?

"I want to hear it directly from your little mouth. Do you like Julia?"

"N n n no. I I I love her. She is wonderful." Timidly came out of his pouted lips.

"Ya? You like this, don't you? I'm finally waking up to see what I've been m m missing." She mimicked her husband's stutter when he got nervous.

He smiled, crossing both his hands on his lap.

"Well? Say it ROBBIE BOBBIE." Anna did not know why her bold cruelty felt so natural and rewarding.

"M m my love, I think she is amazing. It would m m mean so so so much to m m me if if you could spend m m more time with her. I I I think you are are much better since you you have become friends. I I I beg of you. She is a a an incredible good in in influence." A small stain appeared on his pant zipper.

That was all Anna needed. She was convinced that her man was going to follow a much more unique path. With no idea how, she would need to consult with her new mentor.

Pulling into their driveway, Anna placed her hand on

Robbie's pants and rubbed slowly up and down. Leaning in to speak softly in his ear, she said, "I know what you are. I know. And I'm going to help you get better. Ok baby?"

Robbie instantly went rock hard as he struggled to breathe. He was incapable of moving or speaking.

"I said Ok! DO YOU UNDERSTAND ME ROBBIE?"

He nodded with a glazed look on his face.

"There ya go! Good boy. Now, get out of the car, go upstairs and put your little pajamas on like a good little boy. I'm going to call Julia and have a smoke. I'll be up shortly."

Rob got out of the car, struggling to regain any composure. The garage lighting highlighted his erection and pre-cum stains. Shutting his side of the car door, Anna placed one hand over her mouth and the other outstretched, pointing to his 'accident'.

"Oh, look. Your little guy seems to like the new me a lot." She said with a seductive laugh.

Pulling out her phone and the almost empty pack of cigarettes Julia had given her, she lit up and began calling.

"Hello, my love. How is the little man?" Julia responded from the call display.

"Oh, my fucking God! Girl, I fucking love you. I don't know what the fuck you've done to him, or me, but you just changed our marriage. Like, holy fuck!"

Julia laughed on the other end of the phone.

"Well, Anna, this is just the beginning. If you had fun tonight, wait till you see what I have planned for us tomorrow night." She paused, made the sound of a lighter clicking, and took a deep breath before she continued. "I can see you have grown so much in such a short time. That only happens when this lifestyle is your natural home. You remind me of myself."

Anna felt herself feeling emotionally massaged. Julia was close to the same age but seemed to have so much wisdom and knowledge.

"Tell me more, tell me more." Anna's voice sounding like a kid on Christmas Eve.

"Tomorrow, we're going to Club X. No questions asked."

Anna had only one.

"When you say 'we', do you mean the two of us or all four of us?"

Julia hesitated to respond.

"Just the girls...babe," she said as she exhaled.

Anna ended the call and made her way up to bed. Her husband was on the bed naked and at full attention.

"What's this?" She asked entering the room.

"I gotta fuck you right here, right now."

"Oh my, I don't think I've ever seen you this excited. It's about time!" Anna said.

Rob stood up, slowly unzipped her skirt, and began nibbling her neck.

She turned and dropped to her knees. His cock was still leaking pre-cum as she placed her lips over his head. She looked up as her head moved back and forth. It filled his face with ecstasy.

Anna quickly stood up, pushed him on the bed, and mounted him like her life depended on it. Her slim, manicured hand guided him. Sliding front to back, she could feel him throbbing. She looked him in the eyes and whispered.

"You like the bad girl me, don't you?"

He tried so hard to say something, anything.

"Oh, oh, oh my goooooood!" Was all he could muster.

His cock went from a thick piece of wood to a deflated lump of skin in seconds.

Anna could feel his juices slowly drip down her legs.

"That's it? Seriously?" She looked at him with major frustration.

"I'm sorry, Hunny. But that was fun. It really turned me on. Your friend though, she's a real piece of work. What a bitch."

Anna opened her mouth and scrunched her eyelids.

"What? But you said you liked her?"

"I was just playing along. I can't stand her. I like this side of you but ya, not so much for that woman."

"I see. So now that you've got your rocks off, 'the game' is over for you?"

Rob stood up to pull the covers up onto the bed.

"Yes. My original position still stands. I think she has got her nose in places it does not belong."

It pissed her off. She felt used and played by her husband.

"Listen, Robert, I'm going out to a club with Julia tomorrow night. Deal with it."

She turned her night table light off and turned to have her back facing her husband.

CHAPTER EIGHT

he weekend morning ritual was awkward. Robert was downstairs pouring from a fresh brew as Anna entered the kitchen.

"Good morning, my love." He said.

"Don't talk to me. Last night was not a game. I'm going out with Julia tonight. A girl's night out. I'm fed up with our boring life. I don't want to speak to you right now."

Robert raised both hands in the air to signify he would not provide any objections.

Texting to Julia throughout the day, Anna felt embarrassed explaining the sudden turn of events. Her responses were consoling, indicating to Anna that her actions were a typical newbie mistake. Meet-up time, place, and what to wear became the balance of correspondence.

At 7 pm Robert asked when dinner was being served.

"Um, I have no idea. You're on your own. I'm meeting

Julia for dinner, drinks and then we're going to a dance club. Have fun." She slammed the door on the way out.

The drive took Anna past several strip plazas before arriving at the bar. For the first time in ten years, she reclaimed her independence and pulled into a plaza with a 24/7 variety store to buy herself a package of her own cigarettes. 14 minutes later, she was at the bar where Julia waited in her car.

"Hello, my love," Julia said as she got out of her car and went to hug Anna.

"I fucked up. I mean, I seriously fucked up, didn't I?" Anna blurted as Julia got closer.

"No. Not at all. Yes, you made a mistake, but it won't matter in a week or two. Trust me. Tonight, I'm about to introduce you to a world you have no idea about. If you listen to me and do exactly as I say, you will discover your inner Goddess. That's what you really want, isn't it?"

"More than anything in this world. Yes!" Anna replied.

The two women left their cars and headed into a top-shelf restaurant and bar with the windows blacked out. They greeted Julia at the door by name.

"Good evening, Miss Julia. Is this a lovely Unicorn you're gracing us with, this fine evening?"

"No. This is my best friend. You can call her Miss Anna."

Anna looked to Julia with a contorted face.

"What's with the Miss this and Miss that?" Anna asked.

"Oh my love, I'm about to turn your universe into a fairytale. You'll see."

Once they were seated, Anna pulled her cigarettes out. Julia noticed immediately.

"I'm impressed! Now you have your own? Good for you. Say bye-bye to the goody- two-shoes Anna." As she raised her glass in a toast with Anna.

"So what did I do wrong, Julia? You had my husband in the palm of your hands. Like he was your puppet. He stayed like that with me on the drive home, and then, pooof, he became Mr. Dicksmack. Because I put out?"

Julia waited for the server to take their order before responding.

"So, Anna, let me explain. I'm positive your husband, and that for the record, this is the last time either of us should call him that. Your hubby is a true cuckold. They are the absolute best thing any woman could ever ask for."

"I kind of thought he might be after I saw how he got with your head games. But..."

"But what?" Julia said. "Cuckolds have no control over their headspace UNLESS they get off. As long as they are 'in need', absolutely EVERYTHING you say and do is magically wonderful." Julia said with indefinable sexuality to her body motion.

"Are you telling me I can never let my husband, I mean hubby get off?"

Julia bit her lower lip as she waited for the already anticipated question.

"Wellllll, not quite. As you get more experienced, you'll learn when and how often you can let him release. For the early stages, however, yes. I would not please him for at least two months."

"What? He'll go postal"

"No, he won't. Besides, we can always allow him to please himself in the early days. Baby steps, my love. Baby steps."

Anna looked and felt apprehensive. Perhaps this was too much for her and Robert, she thought to herself.

"Julia, you're scaring me. I just want to have some fun and get back some control in our marriage. I don't want to flat out torture the poor man, I mean..."

"Anna, listen to me. Bobbie. No, let's call him little bobbies for now. Little bobbies is a cuckold. I know what I'm talking about. I was very mean and condescending to him last night. You continued that on in your car. How was he when you felt his cock? How did he fuck you when you went upstairs?"

Anna sipped her glass of wine as she contemplated Julia's words. Before she could respond, the wait staff arrived with their entrees. The music slowly increased in volume and beats as they waited for their desserts.

"Julia, yes, Robbie. I mean, little bobbies was the horniest I have ever seen him. But I think he just wanted to see the bad girl me. Depriving him of sex, that's just cruel."

"We will see my love. We will see. Tonight is an experiment for the two of you, only neither of you know it yet."

Anna lifted her right eyebrow in curiosity.

"What? Oh, Julia, I like your devilish side, but I'm kinda nervous. What do you have planned here?"

Almost timed perfectly, the lights dimmed as the music went to full club mode. The wait staff hurriedly went from table to table removing the tableware as an entire wall rolled up, offering a way to the second half of the establishment, laser lights and all.

"Welcome to the club X, my love," Julia shouted over the music.

Up till this point, Anna paid no attention to the other guests. They filled it with couples slightly older than one would expect in a dance club. Additionally, there seemed to be only one or two single ladies, but at least two dozen men that most women would give their left arm to be with.

"What the hell is this place?" Anna asked.

Julia gestured to the now exposed 'dance section' of the establishment. There was a round piece of furniture resembling a bed in the center of the dance floor, with multiple more private seating areas along the perimeter, separated with sheer curtains.

"Tonight, you watch. You smell. You believe. Soon, you do." Julia said with the biggest smile, slowly letting smoke exhale from her mouth.

Anna's heart pounded. She was scared about what she was about to expose herself to. She also felt enveloped in a cozy, warm blanket of evil. She struggled to fight how good it felt. The alcohol was doing its job. She wanted more.

By 3 am, the two women had dirty danced with several young men. The room was filled with euphoric smells of sex. Anna had now watched another woman give a blowjob to three men at the same time. She had witnessed a husband kiss his wife with passionate love as she was getting pounded by another man from behind. IT WAS AMAZING. Anna could feel the moistness between her legs as she watched in admiration.

Heading back to their cars, both women no longer had the buzz from the alcohol. Anna's ears were ringing as Julia said some parting words.

"Okay Anna, this is exactly what I want you to say and

do with little bobbies when you see him in the morning." Julia started a checklist of words and actions Anna was to take.

CHAPTER NINE

*a*nna could smell bacon cooking as she opened her eyes. Struggling to focus her vision, the LED clock looked like it said 1:17. The bedroom filled with bright afternoon sunlight as she sprang out of bed. She slipped on some track pants, an old T-shirt, and some socks before going downstairs. The house was silent except for the frying sound in the kitchen.

"Good morning, Anna. You must have got home really late." Rob said.

Anna was in no mood to be sociable at any level. Her head was pounding from over-sleeping, a mild hangover, and no coffee in her bloodstream.

"meehhhh," was all that she could produce as a response.

Robert stood by the stove, making an elaborate brunch for the two of them. This was very uncharacteristic of him. He poured a fresh mug of coffee and passed it to his wife before she asked.

"Thanks," Anna said in a glib tone.

"Your very welcome, my dear. Brunch will be ready in about 10 minutes. Both kids had a sleepover at a friend's last night, so we have the house all to ourselves for now. How are you?"

As Anna sipped her coffee, she randomly thought how wonderful a cigarette would go with the coffee, when she realized her husband was talking to her.

"What? I'm sorry, what did you say?"

"I asked how you are feeling? My goodness, you must have had a good time with your friend last night. You look rough." Robert said.

Anna remembered the evening. What she did. What she saw, and what Julia told her, she must do now. She remained quiet and distant from her husband as she ate her brunch. Her eyes remained down at the plate or looking out the window throughout the meal.

"Anna, is everything ok? I mean with us. We had some hostile words last night and then you left and now you're giving me the silent treatment. Talk to me."

Anna smiled as she lifted her mug to take a last sip. Putting it down, she spoke.

"Robbie, close the kitchen blinds."

He looked at her, unsure what was going on. The blinds were closed.

"Good boy. Now, stand over here" She pointed to the middle of the kitchen floor away from any counter, table, or chairs. He moved with reluctance.

"Good. Now, take all your clothes off."

"What the fuck? Anna, I know our little thing last night was fun, but where are you going with this?"

Anna grinned but remained silent as she used her hands to show he should continue and remove all his clothes as instructed. The smile on his face suggested he thought she was about to blow him.

"Okay, there. Now what? Are you gonna use your mouth or aren't you going to get naked also?" He said.

She remained silent and as her eyes surveyed him from top to bottom. She stood up, turned the chair she was in backward, and remounted facing him with her chin resting on the back of the chair.

"Ok, Robbie. Here's what we're going to do. I'm going to talk and you're going to speak only when told to do so. DO YOU UNDERSTAND?"

He nodded. His face screaming anticipation of some form of sexual gratification.

"Good boy. So last night, Julia and I went to a sex club."

"What?" Robert blasted.

"HEY! Shut the fuck up. I told you, you say nothing."

"But Anna, you're getting me worried. Hurry and say what you're gonna say and blow me, please."

Anna looked at him with disgust.

"Listen, robbie, I said shut the fuck up. Speak again and you will never hear my voice."

Fear and anxiousness took over his facial and body expressions.

"Again, last night Julia and I went to a sex club. I saw wonderful things robbie. I mean really wonderful things. Does that bother you, that I saw wonderful things robbie?"

He kept his mouth shut and nodded. Anna noticed his cock was not hard, but it looked a little bigger than 2 minutes earlier.

"Oh, it bothers you, little robbie? I'm sorry, baby. But I didn't just see, I could smell wonderful things. It filled the room with sex. It was so magical, ya know what I mean? I even started getting a little wet. Does that bother you, little robbie?"

He nodded again. His cock was now an elevator on its way up. As she continued and could see he was responding exactly as she expected, her desire continued increasing.

"I'm not done. I not only saw things and smelled wonderful things, but I also wanted to do things. Really, really, really, bad and wonderful things. Do you know what I wanted to do, little robbie bobbie?"

He turned his head from side to side. His cock was almost at full attention. She pointed to it.

"Oh, look, little bobbies seems to like where I'm going. Well, let me tell you, I wanted to fuck... but I didn't do that little robbie bobbie. No, no, no. I did not do that."

Like a stopwatch, his cock slowly went down a floor or two.

"No, I did not fuck anyone. I did some dirty dancing with some really hot young guys though." She paused for dramatic effect. "And do you know what, I could feel their rock hard cocks trying to burst through their pants. Screaming to get inside me. It was wonderful."

Once again, his cock was back at full attention.

"And do you know what, little robbie bobbie? I really wanted to fuck them. I wanted to feel them deep inside me. I mean, they felt so big and hard."

She then stood up, walked over to Rob, and put his

cock in her hand without making any stroking motions. He looked at her with baby eyes. The same eyes he had when Julia spoke to him at the restaurant.

"You see this, little bobbies. This is really unacceptable. I know it. You know it. It also says little bobbies here also likes the idea of me being fucked hard. Don't you think?"

Robbie remained silent but agreed with another nod. Anna could not believe she was being so cruel to her husband. She was sure she would feel guilt, but she could see her husband was enjoying her cruelty. She continued.

"Do you agree with me? You agree that your little cock is not good enough for me?"

He nodded.

"No, no, no. Now I want my little robbie bobbie to speak."

"Yes, dear."

"Yes, dear what?"

"Yes dear, my cock is too small to satisfy you."

It filled Anna with a rush of power. The last time she felt this way was in her young adulthood when she dabbled with cocaine.

"Good little boy. So you understand I want to fuck younger, bigger, harder cocks. Is that correct, my little robbie bobbies?"

"Yes, dear." Rob could barely speak. His cock was beyond 90 degrees.

"Wonderful. And because you love me so, so, so much, you now realize that I need to fuck other guys. Yes?"

"Yes, dear."

She gave him a soft kiss on the lips, crept to his ear,

and whispered as she slid her hand back and forth on the shaft of his cock.

"And you want me to fuck other guys, don't you?"

"Yes, dear."

"Oh, look at that. Your little bobbies is letting out some pre-cum. I want to hear you say it. Say you want me to fuck other men. It's ok little bobbies, your tiny cock has already told the truth, but I want to hear it from your baby mouth."

His body was trembling with excitement.

"I want you to fuck other men, dear"

She gave a light, evil little laugh.

"Listen, little bobbies. You still don't get this. I am not your fucking dear. I am now your Goddess. And your Goddess wants to hear you beg. I want you to beg me to fuck other men. I want to hear you say you're small and I want you to know I'm not getting you off today. SAY IT!"

"I I I beg you. I'm begging you. Please. I admit it. I desperately want to see you fuck other men. I I I know that I I... I have a small dick and and and you deserve so much more You are my my my Goddess. I'm begging you. Please"

"Oh, what a good little boy bobbies is today. Okay, now that we understand each other, get dressed. I'm going into the garage to have a cigarette."

Anna grabbed his chin, turned his head to face her directly. Giving him a peck on his nose, looked into his eyes and left the kitchen, leaving him standing naked, erect, and completely unsatisfied.

CHAPTER TEN

"*H*ello, my love. Have you spoken to him yet?" Julia said into the phone.

"OH MY FUCKING GOD!" Anna said as she exhaled. She could hear Julia laughing on the other end of the call.

"I told you, girl. Now you have to be strong. Trust me, this is going to get challenging for a while."

"Wait, what? What do you mean?" Anna asked.

"Oh my love, so much to learn. So much. Today is Saturday. A good friend of mine is having a cuck house party. Tonight, you're going to seal the deal with your little bobbies."

"You mean you think I should fuck another man? I don't know if Rob... I mean bobbies will be ready for that." Anna said with a heavy sigh, following.

"Oh, you're right. He's not ready. That's why we are going to make him 'ready'".

"Julia, I love this power and control, but I just feel so guilty. I don't know if I should take things all the way here."

"Anna, do you love bobbies?"

"Of course I do. He has been an amazing provider to me and my children."

"I see. And his cock. What does his cock say about you being with other men?"

"Welllll, you're right on that account. Fuck, I felt so bad at first, but his little dick was loving it."

"EXACTLY! If you love him, you will do what's right for him, and what's right for you. He wants this. You want this. He just can't bring himself to push you into it."

"So, by fucking other men, I'm actually showing that I love him even more? Is that what you're saying?" Anna asked.

"Do you have a pen? Here are the details." Julia then gave Anna the address, time, and dress code.

Turning back into the house, Anna extinguished her cigarette. She returned to an empty kitchen. The water was running from the shower upstairs. Alarm bells went off in her head. Taking two steps at a time, she ran up the stairs, burst open the bathroom door, and ripped the shower curtain open.

There bobbies was. Cock in hand.

"DON'T YOU FUCKING DARE!" She yelled.

He was just about to climax when she grabbed his hand and ripped it away. He was embarrassed but more in fear from the shock.

"I I I I'm s s s sorry dear." Bobbies was almost incapable of speaking with a wave of mixed emotions.

"Again, I'm not your dear. I am your Goddess. Under

no circumstances are you to please yourself. Get out of the shower and get dressed."

His cock went limp immediately after the shock. He cowered out of the shower to dry off. Anna could not believe herself. She had no idea where her behavior was coming from. It scared her, how natural it came to her.

"Now listen, I've spoken to Julia. We are going out again tonight. You are to join us. This is not optional. I'm not asking. Get yourself dressed and let's get started with the grocery shopping so we're not rushed getting ready."

"Okay."

"OKAY WHAT?" She barked.

"O O OKAY, my Goddess."

The power control and complete dominance was intoxicating. Anna, yet again, felt a dampness between her legs.

CHAPTER ELEVEN

The moon was cloud covered in the night sky. As Anna and bobbies left the house, it seemed darker than normal. She wore skintight black leather pants, a strapless low cut top, and stilettos that made her taller than her husband. He was 'instructed' to wear jeans that were now too short, and a dress shirt, buttoned all the way, with no tie. He both looked and felt like an idiot. They took his BMW so he could drive while she worked on him.

"But I don't know where we are going." Bobbies said.

"Just shut the fuck up and drive BOBBIE." She giggled hearing herself call her husband 'bobbies'.

"I enjoy calling you 'bobbies'. It sounds cute. Ya know, like is bobbies a little boy or a little girl, kinda funny and cute. You love that, don't you? You like being called bobbies."

She moved her hand to his lap. His cock was very

much present. Wanting to capitalize on the moment, she rubbed in an unfocused direction to frustrate him more.

"Y Y Yes, my Goddess."

"Now tell me again, bobbies. Tell me you want me to fuck real men. I want to hear you say it one more time."

His cock went from zero to hero, solid.

"I do, m m my Goddess."

"Good, cause we're almost there."

They pulled the car to the curbside, in front of 4 other cars. Anna waited for her husband to exit and offer to open her side. She had a cigarette ready to light as she got out. She could not believe the shift in their relationship in just over a week. The reality of what was about to potentially happen slammed her in the face. Each drag was deep and aggressive. She was nervous. Was this just a fantasy they were both living out or was this about to end their marriage?

"HELLO, my loves." Julia came bouncing out the front door.

Discretely, Anna turned to her new friend and told her about the unexpected cold feet.

"Oh love, trust me. You and bobbies are way past the point of no return. This should excite both of you. You should be happy, not scared. Isn't that right, my little kitten?" She said as she turned to bobbies.

"Y Y Yes J J Julia." Bobbies said anxiously.

"Come inside, Miss Anna, and bring your little bobbies so he can meet his little playmates." Julia placing her hand behind Anna, giving her a gentle push to enter the threshold of the residence.

The sound of deep bass music was coming from downstairs. A strong and distinct odor of weed hung in the air.

The entire main floor was lit by candles, offering only silhouettes of the guests.

Julia's husband, fluffy took bobbies hand and pulled him to the side to offer some comfort and provide some distinct separation between him and Anna.

"Here love, you look like you could use some of this. The really good stuff is downstairs, but we can get to that once you've loosened up more." Julia said as she passed a bong for Anna to inhale.

Anna looked across the room to see if her husband was looking, but all she saw was darkness. Two deep hauls, some uncontrolled coughs, and a few laughs later, Anna was feeling just fine.

"Now, do you like chocolate or vanilla, my love," Julia asked as they went down the stairs.

"Ice cream? Cake? What do you mean?" Anna innocently asked.

"You tell me?" Julia swept her hand out to a room filled with 6 shirtless men. All in their early 30s. All dreamy. Three were Caucasian and three were black. Anna's face looked like a little girl on Christmas morning.

"Oh my. This is wonderful, Julia. So, um, aaah, how does this work? I don't want to do anything unless I can see my husband's face to know he's okay with it."

"N n n nooo. You don't get to do that, my love. We have taken care of your bobbies. We will make sure he is a part of the action, but not until you're ready yourself. Go grab a drink at the bar, talk to the men. If you like one, tell him you like him and he'll take care of everything else. That's all you need to know."

Anna could feel a low-level panic that seemed to be subdued only by the weed and the raging sexual desires she felt deprived of for so many years. Her inner needs forcing her to move forward, she approached the bar and ordered two double shooters and a Long Island iced tea.

An hour later she could feel the alcohol and weed softening her apprehensions. It was a welcomed surprise. A conversation with Brad, a muscular black man, was nice. There was a connection in their dialogue. Suddenly, he asked if she would mind if he kissed her.

"Umm, I guess so," Anna said bashfully.

His scent was distinct with pheromones that screamed manliness. His hands slid down to her thighs as he nibbled her earlobe. She looked over his shoulder to see Julia lying on a couch with one man on his knees and his face buried in between her legs. Another man stood as Julia sucked him with great enthusiasm. Anna returned to the moment.

She brought her own hands down to Brad's ass. She could feel the power in this young man's body. He was a sexual organism. Every fiber of his being exuded sexuality. Her hands crept up to his chest as his hands found the moistness between her legs. She spread to allow him greater access. His chest was smooth and muscular. Anna wanted more of this man.

Seamlessly, she moved her hands down. Down. Down. Not sure when he did it, Brad had conveniently undone his pant buttons and zipper. Anna's hand slid effortlessly underneath his pants. Down.

And there it was. A huge, hard, throbbing cock. Stroking it became next to impossible. It was so big; it occupied most of the room under his pants.

"Fuck it, I need these off you now." She whispered into his ear.

He pushed her away and placed his index finger to his lips to be quiet.

"First, sexy lady, let's crank this party up a notch." He said as he grabbed a silver tray from the bar ledge. On top were 8 elegant lines of white powder and a straw. Anna looked at him with joy. She picked up the straw and did a line without a second of hesitation. The taste in the back of her throat. The rush of energy. It felt so good inside. She looked up at his smiling face.

"Ya, that's what I'm talkin bout baby. Now on your knees and suck."

Anna loved everything about this. He was in charge. Finally, someone was going to please her the way she deserved.

Dropping to her knees, she did not want this man to be anything but hard. Her tongue. Her lips. She made every motion like her life depended on it. She wanted this piece of him deep inside her. Her left hand went down to rub her clitoris. Her thongs were soaked with anticipation. She could wait no longer.

Standing up, Anna launched her tongue into Brad's mouth. The young man pushed her away and offered her some more white powder. Her eyes opened wide with excitement. Slapping her ass, he then quickly turned her around and guided her to bend over. Anna was tingling in every part of her existence. She could feel his cock searching desperately. Searching.

He ripped her leather pants down and slowly eased his cock in. Deeper. Deeper. It filled her with a real man. Placing both her hands on the back of the couch for support, she turned around to look at him. He still had half his cock unused.

"You like that, baby?" Brad asked.

Anna's eyes were closed. She was almost having an orgasm just from the body buzz.

She opened her eyes to respond. There he was. Standing at the bottom of the stairs was her husband. His face looked confused. His right hand aggressively stroking the cock sticking out of his pant zipper.

"Yesss!" Anna moaned. "You feel soooo good. Fuck me. HARD!"

She could not help herself. She felt omnipotent. Bobbie blew her a kiss and mouthed the words "I love you so much, my Goddess". That was all Anna needed. She let go of any final inhibitions.

Brad's large, powerful hands grabbed her hips and thrust her into himself. Anna could feel the complete and total dominance this man had. His cock never losing its rhythm or rigidness. The sweat between their bodies accentuated the sliding motions in every position they did.

Anna had lost complete track of time when Brad stopped and said he wanted to reload.

"Holy shit. You're a machine, young man. Can I have some more of that?" She pointed to the tray. Brad winked.

"That's my baby girl." He said.

Three minutes later, Brad returned the tray to the bar, and lay down. Without prompting, Anna used her lips to their fullest. He was at full attention before she had a chance to suck.

That was all she needed.

CHAPTER TWELVE

*A*nna sat up, lifted one leg over his firm chest, and slowly guided his cock back into its new home. She could feel every throbbing inch as it re-entered. She had lost count of how many times it brought her to the edge of heaven. This time, she had the control, the pace.

Sliding back and forth, up and down, she looked into Brad's dark brown eyes. It felt so good to be with a real man. So good. Soooo goooood. Their bodies were in perfect timing. With the power of each thrust, Anna never wanted this to end. He was the perfect male specimen. His body was made to fuck. Tonight, Anna could feel, she too, was made to fuck.

The pleasure grew. She was losing her thoughts. The pleasure was...

"OH MY GOD. YES! YES! YES! FUUUUUCK! YES!"

Anna felt something she had not felt for a long time.

Her body convulsed with sensations that felt better than anything she had ever felt before. A tidal wave of joy and release took over. A puddle of liquid fell between her legs.

She was truly satisfied.

Brad tapped her ass. "Okay, baby girl. I's gots ta go." As he glanced at his watch.

"What time is it?" Anna asked him.

He smiled and shifted his arm so she could see the time.

"What! 3:37 AM. That can't be."

"Ya baby, dats da time. Hope your hubby is still here."

Anna suddenly realized her surroundings. Julia and her boy toys were gone. Bobbies was no longer at the stairs. She became concerned about what would happen now.

She looked in the bar mirror. Her hair was a mess. Her leather pants were haphazardly lying on the floor, with one shoe on top, the other flung into the corner. Trying to move as quickly as possible, Anna made herself look semi presentable and ran up the stairs.

Sitting at the kitchen table were several couples, including bobbies. Anna could not look her husband directly in the face. It filled her with guilt and disgust in her actions. She had taken this little game too far. Julia could see the look on Anna's face.

Scratching the chair as she got up, she went to Anna.

"Hello, my love. Come. Come with me. We need to have a girl talk. Sorry girls" Julia said to the group of both men and women sitting around.

Julia briskly moved Anna outside the house, lit two cigarettes, and passed one to Anna.

"Good girl, Anna. I am so proud of you."

"Julia, I think I've just made a huge mistake. I'm so

embarrassed. I can't even look at Robert. Is he upset? I mean, is he ever going to forgive me?"

"Relax, Anna. It's all good. Little bobbies is just a cutesie pie. He'll be fine."

"But, how is he? What did he say?"

"Nothing that you need to worry yourself about my love. Just the typical cuckold angst bullshit stuff. Y'know, feeling sorry for himself. Feeling like he is not good enough for you."

Anna felt her husbands' pain. Her eyes filled with tears.

"Hey! Anna, stop that right now. Little bobbies is going through what all little cucky's go through. It's ok. It's good actually. He loves you and it does not upset him what you did at all."

"No? He must be livid." Anna said.

"My love, you are still new to being a Goddess. Um, the proper term is Cuckoldress. Right now, you have him exactly where you want and he needs to be."

"What?"

"Girlfriend, you still do not know the fun you and I are going to get up to. This is just the beginning. Your little cucky husband LOVED, L O V E D IT! Now, you need to keep face and carry on as his Goddess."

"More? Are you saying I could have even more fun than I did tonight?" Anna said as she took a long drag and had the devilish look sweep over her face, almost instantly forgetting any guilt she had.

"My love, we are now officially besties. Let's talk about the training program little bobbies needs to start, first thing in the morning. Have you ever heard of a cock cage...?"

THE MENTOR 2
THE INFLUENCE GETS STRONGER

Allora Sinclair

A Cuckoldress Is Born

ALSO BY ALLORA SINCLAIR

ABOUT THE AUTHOR

ABOUT THE AUTHOR

 Allora Sinclair is a happily married 40 year old mom. She and her loving cuckold husband Dave (davie) have been in a cuckold marriage for over seven years and she has now decided to start documenting their journey. If Allora is not found at her computer or our shopping for a new pair of shoes, she is usually found in the caring arms of davie or embraced in ecstasy with one of her favorite bulls. She has done a series of non-fiction books to help couples navigate their way through the heavily distorted life of being a cuckold couple. She is now working on a series of fiction books that are loosely based on some of their real-life adventures. This story would be one.